A

SOULLESS

WHITE

SHROUD

BY: TRE GARCIA

A

SOULLESS

WHITE

SHROUD

BY: TRE GARCIA

A SOULLESS WHITE SHROUD

FIRST EDITION

ISBN-9780998040042 (Print Version)

To my Dad and Tio Raul, thank you for teaching me the beauty of our people and culture.

To my Mom, thank you for being my pillar of strength.

ABOLISH ICE!

TABLE OF CONTENTS

CHAPTER I

GUADALUPE DOMÍNGUEZ

Life served nothing for Guadalupe Domínguez. Raised in despair, she spent every day of her life in the same redundant cycle that was expected of a woman living in a drug-infested slum.

As a little girl, she never experienced schooling, hijinks, or any whimsical pleasures that children from more prosperous places knew. For Guadalupe, her aged, hardened, scarred fingers told the stories of her endless days working in fields where she and her family toiled for meager wages.

The idea of dreams and hopes were never a concept for Guadalupe, as she may have envisioned a family in a modest home but would never come close to such a fairy tale.

Guadalupe came from a once proud, humble town named Soliz that provided vibrant grapefruit and oranges to neighboring larger cities. Her generation would be the last to be raised in such a climate. The drug cartels would use the village as a pass-through, leading to an influx of gangs and violence, causing the orchards to become parched, never to grow again. The once-luminous Soliz drained all life and became a gray, overcrowded slum resembling other Central American dystopias.

Guadalupe would grow up having to fend for herself and then for her two children, Juanito and Ignacio. Juanito came from a man who paid for a desperate Guadalupe, only to never be seen again. Brokenhearted, she withered away her entire youth to raise her first son.

Eight years later, the conception of Ignacio came when she thought she finally met the man whom she assumed would take her out of Soliz, only to leave her after being told she'd be bearing his child.

Guadalupe would raise Juanito, and soon add Ignacio, in a dirt-floor, rusted-tin shack, in a time when death and murder ran rampant in their decaying streets, empty orchards, and blood-soaked alleyways.

Guadalupe, a heavy-set woman whose age does not resemble her tired-worn exterior, had rock-like feet and vacant toenails that were lost during the fall of Soliz. Although her legs were sturdy and as strong as a woman who lived her entire life in defense, Guadalupe walked with a cadence of each foot barely lifting from the ground, as if she were conserving her steps for one final unannounced effort for life—it was clear, patience was all she knew.

Despite appearing aged beyond her years, to the steady eye, anyone could see what beauty she may have had if raised in a nurtured environment.

Guadalupe spent every day the same: she awoke just before dawn and awaited her ancient God to rise to its full glory. Her first meal included a half-stale tortilla and boiled clean rainwater she made the night before from a dug hole in the center of her rusted-tin shack in a handle-less pot she found years ago in the Soliz landfill she often frequented. After consuming her half-cold, stale tortilla, she always made sure to leave the other half for Juanito.

As for Juanito, he spent his day gaining free education in the slums of Soliz, hoping to come home alive, which, of course, was a constant stream of worry for Guadalupe.

Before her ancient God became too unbearable, she'd put Ignacio in a dingy sling made from an old dress, tie it around her back, and make the journey to the Soliz dump, known as *La Chureca,* which the town had inherited from the neighboring city of Balboa.

***

As Guadalupe approached *La Chureca,* she admired its overwhelming presence, resembling a man-made mountain range of trash and despair. She spent her mornings pillaging through rotted waste, syringes, stacked animal carcasses, and soiled life.

She, along with everyone else from the dystopia of Soliz, plundered in hopes of finding anything of substance to feed their flock. Since the people of Soliz were left to fend for themselves or become absolved by the passing drug paraphernalia, most of the elder generation would choose a life amongst the soiled hills, knowing they'd be buried in the fields they had once proudly occupied.

Amid the buzzing from the horseflies, the reeking smell of dehydrated death, or the constant crackling from the paper trash that consumed the dump, the conversation amongst the once proud people of Soliz always remained the same:

**"LA LEYENDA DE ROGELIO ALANIZ–
EL HIJO DE SOLIZ."**

CHAPTER II

MR. HERRERA'S SHADED DOTTED WALL

Rogelio Alaniz began as a simple man, only to rise as a hero and the pulse of Soliz's final great generation. Raised in a loving embrace from the sandy soil of Soliz, Rogelio grew up in a time where community and modest prosperity united the silhouettes from the eventual emptiness that would later consume them.

The shift from vibrance to despair in Soliz happened in a single, pivotal moment. The largest citrus distributor in Soliz at the time, *Herrera's Farms,* abruptly closed its doors without warning, causing neighboring purveyors to follow suit, leaving their humble workers to fend for themselves.

What happened to the owner of the once-proud grove where Rogelio had worked since childhood echoed through Soliz, causing neighboring towns to worry and, for the first time, confront the unknown.

The people of Soliz inherited their religion and language from European influences centuries ago, but because their hands were shaped by nature, their ancient Gods had always flowed through their veins, providing life. If a gray overcast appeared, it was welcomed as a sign of a cooler day to pick crops and, most likely, provide fresh rain to nourish their grove.

But on this specific day, a looming cloud cover wasn't like most. It buried the sun in darkness, causing the workers of *Herrera's Farms* to stop and look up at the sky in unease, and most of all, in fear. As the pitch-dark sky inhaled any light, the workers held onto their loved ones.

Rogelio, alone, removed his work gloves and admired the dark clouds receding as the sky shifted to a pale ash—like a slab of freshly poured concrete. The sky would eventually lighten but remain dreadful as all the laborers would go back to work as if they knew whatever phenomenon had just occurred was expected.

***

That following morning, the sad clouds remained and loomed over Soliz without ever giving a drop of rain. Before the workers could begin their day, Mr. Herrera, the owner of *Herrera's Farms*, stopped everyone and told them *"No hay trabajo disponible."* In a stern but vulnerable voice. The workers looked toward the groves and saw an abundance of citrus ready for picking, then back again at him, confused. Mr. Herrera appeared emotionally wounded, his eyes ringed with lines of blood. The laborers whispered amongst themselves, worried.

"Hay una emergencia familiar," Mr. Herrera finally said.

He assured them he would let them know when it was okay to work again. His voice cracked, like a pubescent male teenager, as he signaled his workers to return to their tents. The laborers, including Rogelio, waited patiently, though genuine concern for Mr. Herrera lingered.

***

Although the skies masked the sleepy sun, the merge to night felt endless. The people of Soliz had sincere concern for Mr. Herrera, who had always treated his workers with kindness—unlike his great-grandfather, who had ruled *Herrera's Farms* with an iron fist.

The workers would soon learn that, while Mr. Herrera was away on business, his only child—his son—had been shot and killed in his own home—a tragic prelude to what was to come for Soliz. The last murder in Soliz had occurred a decade before—a love triangle gone wrong.

Days passed without Mr. Herrera stepping out of his home, leaving the citrus fields untouched, rotting, and resembling speckled grit. The workers grew anxious, worried about how to feed their families. Without surprise, they helped one another, feeding each other communally under *Herrera's Farms'* white tents, which resembled snowcaps in the distant mountain terrain.

***

Early one morning, with the moon and sun in transition, Mr. Herrera began packing his truck to leave Soliz. The constant slam of doors and the crunch of his boots against the gravel woke the laborers—including Rogelio, who peeked through the tent's gap to watch Mr. Herrera flee. Half the workers were stunned, murmuring:

"*¿El Sr. Herrera nos deja?*"

The other half, including Rogelio, weren't surprised. After what happened to his only child, they knew he wouldn't stay. Rogelio turned away from the tent crease and instantly noticed the worried eyes of the people who had helped raise him. He realized what he must do.

***

Rogelio walked through the crowd and grabbed his ranchero straw hat. Though worn with shades of grit, it still complemented his dark, chiseled jawline. As he walked barefoot through the grove, he turned back and saw his family standing outside the tent, as if guarding their humble kingdom.

Rogelio stepped onto the owner's paved driveway just as Mr. Herrera came out with a box of garments. Surprised, Mr. Herrera immediately understood that Rogelio sought answers— without a single word being spoken.

Rogelio removed his hat out of respect, pressed it against his heart, and extended his hand. Mr. Herrera rested the box beside the others stacked next to his orange pickup and greeted him.

"*Rogelio, ¿qué puedo hacer por usted?*" he asked.

Rogelio grinned, his patchy mustache standing firm. He pulled his hand back and put his hat back on. It comforted him that Mr. Herrera knew his name despite the hundreds of employees he had.

"*Señor Herrera, primero quiero decirle que lamento mucho su pérdida. Todos estamos profundamente consternados por todo lo que está pasando,*" Rogelio said.

"*Gracias, Rogelio. Aún sigo lidiando con todo, y los tiempos son difíciles,*" Mr. Herrera replied, his voice steady, but his hands trembled.

"*Quiero pedir perdón por haberlos dejado, porque todos ustedes han significado mucho para mí.*" He shook his head, staring past Rogelio as if looking into the future.

"*Pero todo está cambiando aquí en Soliz, y el futuro es tan sombrío como este nuevo cielo. Te recomiendo a ti y a los demás que también se vayan.*"

Rogelio looked up at the tinged sky, hoping for a glimpse of sunshine, but he knew his ancient God had no strength to break through. He wiped his brow with the edge of his sleeve, then faced Mr. Herrera.

"Quería decirle que todos le agradecemos por el trabajo y la vida que ha brindado durante generaciones," Rogelio said, carrying the weight of gratitude passed down like an heirloom as he glanced at his family in the distance.

"Y si puede ver directamente detrás de usted, nuestra familia, sus trabajadores, están de pie con orgullo por el sudor y el amor que hemos puesto en sus campos."

The question loomed between them like the sky above. There was no avoiding it.

"También estamos increíblemente preocupados por lo que traerá el mañana," Rogelio added.

They both looked up at the dreaded sky, appearing worried. Mr. Herrera turned back, grinning as he removed his hat and raised it in salute to his last family. The men guarding the weather-beaten tent raised their hats proudly.

"Mira, sígueme adentro," Mr. Herrera requested.

***

Rogelio stepped into Mr. Herrera's home for the first time. He recalled being a boy, playing fútbol among the field workers. Once, he had to retrieve a ball that had landed near the house. That day, he had met a younger, dapper Mr. Herrera, who had been carrying what would soon be his reason for leaving some twenty-five years later.

Rogelio noticed the emptiness of the home. The wall paint resembled the rustic orange found in Mexican pottery often filled with his citrus. As he turned the corner into the kitchen, his eyes were immediately drawn to a fresh coat of paint, disguising what was likely the spot where Mr. Herrera's son had been shot. Yet, despite the effort, speckled blood remained vivid in its shade.

One could only assume that Mr. Herrera came home to his son's massacre, and rather than worrying about repainting a simple wall, perhaps washing away his son's blood would've been too difficult to ever endure.

Amid small talk, Rogelio couldn't take his eyes off the shaded speckled wall, when Mr. Herrera offered him a drink for which Rogelio would decline.

An awkward silence would ensue when Mr. Herrera would see something inspiring.

"*¡Mira!*" Mr. Herrera said looking outside his living room window.

Rogelio turned his attention from the wall and saw the workers loading Mr. Herrera's truck, a small smile forming on his face. Mr. Herrera then asked Rogelio to stay behind as he excused himself. Rogelio nodded.

He turned back to the freshly painted rustic wall, where he noticed the silhouette of a large cross—one that must have occupied that space for generations. He looked past its shadow and spotted a few faded specks of gray blood freckling its outline.

Without thinking, Rogelio shifted his hat to his other hand and quickly made the sign of the cross.

From a distance, he continued to inspect the wall, his focus drawn to the splattered blood of Mr. Herrera's son as if he were hypnotized. He imagined the moment Mr. Herrera had come home to find his only son lying lifeless on the blood-soaked tile. The thought unsettled him.

The sudden clap of boots against the tile jarred Rogelio from his trance. He quickly shifted his focus away from the wall and straightened his tired, worn shirt just as Mr. Herrera reappeared.

"Rogelio, mira, esto es todo lo que tengo para dar. Comparte este dinero con todos y vete de Soliz," Mr. Herrera said, his voice firm but wounded.

He glanced down at the worn bills in his calloused hands, knowing it wasn't enough, but it was all he had.

"Soliz ya no tiene nada que ofrecer. Todo lo que conocimos de este pueblo, todo lo que alguna vez fue grande, está a punto de desaparecer para siempre," he continued, his gaze distant, as if already seeing the ghost of what Soliz would soon become.

"Y lo que le pasó a mi hijo… es el presagio de lo que nos espera aquí."

Rogelio put the large roll of cash into his pocket without counting and then shook Mr. Herrera's soft hand. As he walked back toward the tent, he glanced over his shoulder and saw Mr. Herrera hang his head over the steering wheel of his old orange truck.

When Rogelio reached the tent, surrounded by laborers, they greeted him with angst and curiosity. After he explained Mr. Herrera's plans, he noticed the faintest trace of hope vanished, replaced by empathy for Mr. Herrera's son—a valid reason, in their eyes, for Mr. Herrera's departure.

Rogelio then remembered the cash and distributed it amongst everyone equally while also keeping his fair share. He walked to his small corner of the large tent, lying down with worries of tomorrow, while praying to never remember Mr. Herrera's shaded dotted wall.

CHAPTER III

"¡ROGELIO! ¡ROGELIO! ¡ROGELIO!"

The night turned day as the morning dew intermingled with the hardened clouds lingering above. Rogelio hadn't slept a wink as thoughts of uncertainty overwhelmed him. All that he had ever known was working the groves. He knew that with the influx of cartels and violence looming, his days would be numbered if he stayed in Soliz.

Rogelio sat up at the edge of his weathered cot and noticed everyone preparing to leave Mr. Herrera's field in defeat. He buried his head in his lap and inhaled. Within that deep breath, a thin beam of light pierced the old, torn tent, shining onto his head as he became enlightened for the first time.

Rogelio's head springs from his lap when he recalled an old story his Tío Oscar once told of an old man from the neighboring town of Balboa escaping to *El Norte*. Rogelio remembered that this old man simply got up one day hungry and desperate and began his odyssey towards a land that he had heard was full of opportunity and life.

Successful in his journey to *El Norte*, people remembered him as *"El Viejo"* — the man who risked it all for the chance of survival.

Rogelio stood from his cot, inspired, and began walking through Mr. Herrera's grove, contemplating what to do next, and whether it would be a good idea to even attempt traveling to *El Norte*. He looked over to the home of Mr. Herrera and considering his oldest son had expired days prior, it seemed like any life that had ever occupied his home had vanished without ever existing.

Rogelio would pull a grapefruit from the vine and cut a portion of the skin from his pocketknife that was given to him by his father at the age of six. As he sucked the pulp from the grapefruit, he dropped it atop the dying soil and realized what he had to do.

Rogelio returned to his cot and began packing when his closest friend, Julio, asked.

"Entonces, ¿qué vas a hacer?"

"Me voy al Norte, Julio." Rogelio answered.

Julio was a life-long friend who, like Rogelio, grew up only in the fields, never traveling past the orchards that he and his family had harvested for many generations.

"¡El Norte!" said Julio elated and confused.

The idea of going to *El Norte* had never even crossed Julio's mind, so hearing Rogelio say he was heading there left Julio quietly wondering.

"¿Qué?" while also being shocked at Rogelio's plan.

"Sí, sí," Rogelio said, pointing towards *El Norte.*

"Nadie va al Norte, especialmente desde Soliz," Julio mumbled, shaking his head.

Rogelio let out a dry laugh. *"Bueno, eso fue antes de que quedáramos absueltos de la vida misma."*

"Se llama 'La Marcha de la Muerte' por una razón, Rogelio," he said, his voice heavy with the weight of countless stories of failure.

"Excepto Balboa, la gente de Álvarez, Zavala y La Mona lo ha intentado, y nunca lo han logrado—ni uno solo, y lo sabes." Julio said.

Both Julio and Rogelio stepped outside the tent, looking toward the direction of *El Norte*, knowing that brave souls always returned as ghosts.

"Ya sé, Julio, pero ni modo, tengo que intentarlo." he said, his voice firm but unsure.

He ran his fingers through the dry earth, searching for something that no longer existed.

"Siempre quise fundirme en la tierra de Soliz como lo hicieron nuestros antepasados, porque esta tierra daba vida. Ahora, es todo menos eso." Rogelio Said.

"¿Y si te traen de vuelta?" Julio said cautiously referring to being caught by the men in green jackets or even worst dead.

"Entonces entiérrame con aquellos que murieron antes de que Soliz se volviera gris." Rogelio said with his chest swelled.

Rogelio would lay down in his small corner of the tent, as Julio looked down on him somewhat proud, which was a new emotion for Julio.

***

Rogelio woke hours later, only to find the large tent empty. After stretching his arms and stifling a yawn, he heard faint murmurs from outside. He quickly put on his boots and hat and stepped out of the tent. Still half-asleep, his eyes widened to the size of the grapefruit he had picked, making him smile.

Everyone from the tent stood proudly in front of Rogelio. Stunned, he greeted everyone. It was evident that Julio shared Rogelio's idea, because many of the women handed him pan dulce, tortillas, and rosaries followed by the sign of the cross on top his head and chest. Streams of tears trickled down his cheeks, falling like droplets onto the groves, as if giving new life to the dying soil.

Rogelio noticed the dark hope they had in their eyes. Although they looked at him with deep admiration and concern, a powerful surge of emotion overwhelmed him—one he had never felt before. Instinctively, he realized he was the chosen one to restore hope. After serving a life of monotony, it was finally time for him to begin his journey toward prosperity and free everyone in Soliz.

Rogelio hugged each person deeply, children included, thanking them for all they had done for him, promising that he would make it to *El Norte.*

After Rogelio packed his bag with the few clothes he owned, Julio then tapped his shoulder from behind.

"Rogelio, sé que estás emocionado por tu viaje, pero entiende—esto significa más que solo encontrar una nueva vida," Julio said, his voice forcibly steady, but the fear of losing Rogelio cracked through.

He placed a hand on Rogelio's shoulder, understanding that he must let go.

"Significa que, si logras llegar a El Norte, nuestro humilde pueblo de Soliz también podrá soñar con ese viaje algún día… y encontrar su propio paraíso."

"Ya sé, Julio, y te lo prometo a ti y a todos aquí que haré todo lo posible para desafiar La Marcha de la Muerte y, por fin, vivir." Rogelio said.

"Por favor, Rogelio, ten cuidado. Todos necesitamos que llegues al otro lado."

Rogelio looked at Julio and understood that his decision was not only for him but for the people of Soliz. As Rogelio put his bag over his shoulder, Julio handed him a gift wrapped in a worn piece of cloth.

"Quiero que tomes esto." he said.

Rogelio anxiously unwraps the gift and it was Julio's machete. *"No, Julio, esto es tuyo. Nunca lo usaste."*

"No, no. Quiero que lo tengas. Tal vez nunca lo usé porque siempre estuvo destinado a ser tuyo." Julio said.

Rogelio held the machete in deep admiration. While looking at the mirror-like blade and the red leather grip handle, he noticed his initials, *R.A.*, engraved just above the guard, likely etched there with Julio's knife. Rogelio rubbed his thumb over the engraving and then hugged him.

"Gracias, hermano. Deberías venir conmigo. Sería mucho más seguro."

"No, no. Quiero estar aquí para la resurrección de Soliz." Julio said.

"Está bien… está bien."

Rogelio stepped out of the tent, and everyone from *Herrera's Farms*, and seemingly the entire town of Soliz, waited for him before he left for *El Norte*. Everyone turned their focus to Rogelio in deep hope. Although Rogelio was shy and not much for speaking out loud, he'd glance over at Julio realizing that he must say something to his people. He suddenly nods, knowing exactly what to say.

"Gracias a todos por su apoyo." Rogelio's voice carried over the gathered crowd, his eyes searching for familiar faces that had shaped his life.

"Llevaré conmigo el espíritu de cada uno de ustedes mientras me adentro en este gran viaje hacia lo desconocido."

He paused, inhaling deeply, as if taking one last breath of Soliz before his fight to save her.

"No sé lo que me espera en La Gran Marcha, pero con su amor incondicional, estoy más que seguro de que llegaré al otro lado." His voice was stern, but the weight of his words pressed heavily on the hopeful hearts of Soliz.

"Y cada día, rezaré para que mi expedición los inspire a encontrarme en la prosperidad."

Rogelio would take a deep pause as his eyes began to swell. Then, a small elder woman who helped raise Rogelio and Julio as children would reach up to him and wipe away his tears marking him in a silent prayer, ending on a sacred rhythm on his forehead.

"*Gracias, Gloría,*" Rogelio said.

"*Diré que tengo miedo de lo que viene, así como ustedes temen por mí,*" he said, his voice steady but with a barely noticeable tremble.

"*Pero sé que debo enfrentar este miedo para poder vivir—para que todos podamos vivir.*" He paused, to absorb the faces before him, each one holding the weight of their own struggles, their own sacrifices.

"*Gracias por criarme, gracias por darme tu fuerza, y sé que Soliz sobrevivirá gracias a todos ustedes.*"

His words pierced through the thick, oppressive air, carried by the same wind that had once whispered stories of resolve, burden, and a defiant spirit.

Rogelio put on his ranchero hat, slung his bag over his shoulder, and walked through the parted crowd he had known his entire life. As he passed, everyone raised a hand over his head and began a communal prayer. In that moment, Rogelio sensed he was ready to take on *La Gran Marcha de la Muerte.* The entire town of Soliz followed Rogelio through the historic streets to the barricaded exit in song and hymn.

Before he took his first steps towards the great march, he'd take one look back, not so much for the people who were watching from afar with hope in their eyes, but take in the only home he had ever known. Rogelio saluted everyone and shouted,

"*¡Gracias, mis hermanos y hermanas!*" Then he looked up to the somber sky, overwhelmed by the reminder of why he must go. Rogelio raised his machete with the red leather grip in the air, as everyone from Soliz would raise their fist, except this time with strength and pride shouting, "*¡ROGELIO! ¡ROGELIO! ¡ROGELIO!*" He drew a deep breath and stepped into the unknown.

CHAPTER IV

ROGELIO ALANIZ–
EL HIJO DE SOLIZ

While the groves of *Herrera's Farms* had been consumed with dried orchards, the final grapefruits were rotting onto the Earth, personifying the once vibrant town of Soliz as its final resting place.

Julio on the other hand had grown restless and wanted to know the status of Rogelio. Julio would often flirt with *La Marcha de la Muerte*, traveling a few kilometers to ask working patrons on the trail if they had seen Rogelio by having to describe him.

Of course, Julio remained unaware of Rogelio's whereabouts, as time became consumed by hope and constant prayer for his bravest friend.

Another place Julio often visited was the cemetery, hoping he would never find Rogelio's body. In neighboring towns like Balboa, La Alvarez, and La Mona, anyone who failed to reach *El Norte* was brought back in the tail of a truck, sometimes in a makeshift casket or wrapped in a white shroud like they were trash that belonged in *La Chureca*.

***

Another month passed, and Julio made his way to the cemetery, hoping he wouldn't find Rogelio there—only to discover a sizable crowd huddled around its entrance. Because Julio saw many familiar faces from *Herrera's Farms*, he bulled his way through the crowd in a deep panic, desperately hoping and praying with rapid breaths that it wasn't Rogelio.

As he'd make his way to the front of the crowd, he'd see a hollow, cold Rogelio wrapped in a soulless white shroud only revealing his trampled face. Julio fell to his knees along with the crowd's desperate cries, which pierced through their whimpers, hoping he'd rise.

The crowd would circle around Rogelio's make-shift casket like an army of ants on a single crumb, then lifted it toward an empty grave without letting it touch the ground, chanting, *"¡ROGELIO! ¡ROGELIO! ¡ROGELIO!"*

The crowd had turned into the entire village of Soliz, marching step by step with the raised casket. People from the outer ring of the crowd would persist through, just to touch Rogelio's casket or toss flowers. Tears coated the newly made trail to his final resting place.

The screams for Rogelio would intertwine with the leery skies, as everyone realized that their newfound hope had died along with Rogelio.

***

Decades later, Rogelio's journey grew into legend, as many from Soliz attempted to conquer *La Marcha de la Muerte*—only to return lifeless and become known as *Los Discípulos de Rogelio's*, a title bestowed upon them by Julio, whose grief never faded.

To this day, his grave is never without floral arrangements and perishables mostly consisting of pan dulce, bottled cerveza, written letters, and rosaries which have christened the top railing of his humble gravestone entitled:

ROGELIO ALANIZ –
EL HIJO DE SOLIZ

CHAPTER V

A LINE IN THE SAND

Because Rogelio's devastating journey was always being babbled amongst Guadalupe's neighbors, many often hesitated for the right time to take the great March. Sadly, for too many, the right time came too late: They either fell into violence or went untreated for illness.

For Guadalupe, that day came when her eldest son Juanito came home bloody and drenched in tears.

He wept against her robust bosom, whimpering as he tried to explain what had happened. Guadalupe soon learned that Chico—Juanito's best friend, had been beaten beyond recognition by one of the countless gangs in Soliz's slums.

The noticeable exhaustion Juanito endured from losing another friend caused him to lose his innocence without realizing that his final day may be sooner rather than later.

Guadalupe would hold Juanito on the ridged corner of their tin shack while also tending to Ignacio —both sons were fast asleep.

Guadalupe stepped outside her shack and saw Chico's grandmother, whimpering as she rocked him back and forth. He was fully wrapped in a spotted, bloodied white shroud.

Having grown immune to such scenes, Guadalupe turned away out of respect and walked toward the edge of the shacks, gazing at the open night sky in deep thought.

For many, living a life with breaks and fortune was never a concept for those in Soliz. Guadalupe always believed that her purpose was for her God and her children. After seeing Juanito in tears, she knew that if she risked another day then she would be like Chico's grandmother rocking away a covered Juanito for the last time.

Guadalupe looked up at the bright dotted sky as if it were her first time, and instinctively pulled out her weathered rosary, and prayed to her creator. With Guadalupe's thumb pressed on the seventh bead of the third decade whispering the Hail Mary, she'd feel a ticklish sensation across her right bare foot.

Startled, she would look down and see a steady stream of ants crossing over the charred hump of her foot and directly to an endless trail. Amused, Guadalupe gently brushed the ants aside and stepped away, admiring their relentlessness.

She then looked up to the proud moon and commenced in the sign of the cross—inspired.

Guadalupe barged through her rusted tin door, waking Juanito. Frightened, Juanito would shuffle from the dirt floor to ask about her urgency so late in the night. She instantly hushed him so he wouldn't wake Ignacio, "*¡Cállate, por favor!*" She'd notice the worrisome eyes from Juanito and brushed his hair back with her hardened hands while gently grazing the slight birthmark on his cheek and say.

"Escucha, necesito que empaques una bolsa pequeña. Nos vamos a El Norte ahora."

"No, Amá, no quiero. Estaré bien." Juanito pleaded. Guadalupe began to question her sudden decision to leave in the middle of the night without being extra careful, but she knew if they didn't leave now than they never would. She pulled Juanito by the arm and whispered in angst.

"¡Yah levántate y vámonos! Agarra tu bolsa y ponle tanta comida como puedas. También lleva esas botellas de plástico vacías, las llenaremos en el camino."

She desperately withheld her tears.

Juanito did as she asked, also grabbing a five-liter bottle half filled with tinged rainwater. With no time lost, they were ready. He carried a small plastic bag filled with shirts and shorts, along with a few empty plastic bottles and a whole bag of cloth diapers that Guadalupe had made for Ignacio to reuse, since she could never afford disposable ones.

Before Guadalupe wrapped Ignacio across her chest, she'd grab a few coins that she had salvaged from *La Chureca*—and left.

Guadalupe would take one last look at their home as they trailed off into town. Although they were leaving many personal items behind, she never wanted to see any of it again. As they walked away, Guadalupe prayed to Saint Christopher, the patron saint of safe travels, crossing herself countless times as they fled Soliz.

Walking past their slum she'd noticed that it was eerily quiet. Although there were a few older men leaning against their shack tired and out of luck, they would let Guadalupe and her family be, as if they knew what leaving at this time of night meant.

While passing through Soliz that reeked of *La Chureca*, they'd also cross the main street that consisted of potholes, cantinas, food carts, drunks, and the newly perishable. Guadalupe held Ignacio as tightly as possible to her chest while also holding onto Juanito's hand, and walk directly to the edge of Soliz in no time—just as she once had as a child.

Like a line in the sand, a single step separated Soliz from the virgin forest. Guadalupe again crossed her chest, and although she feared what was in front of her, she knew she had to be brave for her children.

Gently tugging Juanito's hand, she glanced down at Ignacio's red, sleeping face and smiled. They took their first steps into the dark, grassy forest as though it were second nature.

CHAPTER VI

LA MARCHA DE LA MUERTE

The once-proud moon edged the horizon as Guadalupe, Juanito, and Ignacio moved deeper into the forest. With debris consisting of paper trash, empty plastic bottles, and shreds of clothing coating the battered trail, yet Guadalupe noticed they were completely alone.

She stopped in her tracks to look at both ends curiously, as she assumed the journey towards *El Norte* would be saturated with desperate hungry travelers and families.

Each new thought fueled her nerves, her divot-laden heels scraping the loose gravel and breaking the midnight silence. Guadalupe tried desperately to look ahead at the trail but would only see all but ten feet as the starry night consisted of the only light.

She began to wonder if she had made a mistake, or if she was somehow blessed to have the trail all to herself and her family. Still, she stayed on guard for danger.

"Vamos," Guadalupe said, as they stepped forward.

The early sun rose, following them step by step. While Juanito walked a few steps in front of both his Amá and Ignacio, still, the trail ran vacant. Guadalupe knew that she shouldn't waste any of her energy on being worried, so they continued.

Although the journey might last many weeks, her only plan was to stop briefly to feed her children and then continue without wasting time. She pulled out a tortilla, cut it in half, and handed a piece to Juanito, who turned away so she could feed Ignacio in private.

While feeding Ignacio, Guadalupe surveyed the area to make sure no one was nearby. Still surprised by the silence and the chirp of crickets, she and Juanito would ravish their tortilla in two bites, while Ignacio drank with his eyes closed peacefully.

Guadalupe would grab another stale tortilla and half it once again and seek to find coverage for the night to keep both her sons as comfortable as possible.

Eventually, she would find a large hovering tree surrounded by fragments of litter and slide down the aged trunk to rest. She glanced at Ignacio, kissed his forehead, and whispered a prayer for their safety. As she tended to him, she kept an eye on Juanito, who was eating his tortilla and kicking an empty can in delight.

Guadalupe would smile in serenity for the first time since the first moment she ever held Ignacio months ago, and whispered, *"Gracias, Dios."*

The sky would dim, and she'd look up to the pungent dotted sky that seemed an arm's length away and surrender the night.

***

As the night sky lightened, Guadalupe was stirred by the rustle of leaves. Her eyes, though heavy with exhaustion, widened instantly. A large spotted cat was staring directly into her eyes from a near distance.

She quickly tighten her grip on Ignacio, who was still peacefully sleeping in his aged sling, and on Juanito, who was thankfully fast asleep on her lap.

Guadalupe wanted to cry for help and run to safety, but instead stared directly into the large spotted cat's eyes tranquilly knowing that she could never show fear, while inhaling slowly. The large spotted cat froze in place, unblinking, its squared jaw slightly open to reveal tinged fangs.

Then, suddenly, it scurried away. Guadalupe would exhale in relief but remain guarded until it was out of sight, so she could wake Juanito and get back on the trail.

CHAPTER VII

DEPRIVED SOULS

Countless days had passed, and Guadalupe's feet were consumed with fresh blisters. As her leaky wounds dyed her feet red, she adjusted her stride, walking on the back edge of her callused heels to lessen the pulsing pain.

Juanito began to grow irritated by the monotony of the trail as he ate the stale tortillas his Amá had rationed for this unfamiliar journey—Ignacio was still the perfect passenger.

Guadalupe knew that the key to making this trip as easy as possible was to keep Ignacio kept and fed. While making sure that Juanito was always insight, Guadalupe was grateful to once again have the trail all to herself and at times would have Ignacio latched-on as they continued walking through the burdening heat.

Aware that they were on their last liter of water, they would finally stand parallel to a neighboring slum. Guadalupe knew that they may be able to nourish themselves by using the few pesos she was able to gather to refill their liters. They approached the slum with cautious steps.

Similar to Guadalupe's village, it was drenched in deficiency, as it also reeked of the landfill that she was all too familiar with. Strangely inspired, Guadalupe was reminded of what she left behind and walked into the slum with the intention of leaving.

***

Walking through the busy main street that resembled Soliz, Guadalupe would clutch on to Ignacio as they weaved through the oncoming clutter of pedestrians as her eyes widened. In search for water, all that seemed to be available were the pot-holes consisting of murky pools of sludge only to be occupied with beaten and disheveled dogs flipping their tongues in thirst like a boxer's speed bag.

Guadalupe began to tremble in fear, resisting the urge to cry as she questioned her lack of plans for their great escape. She recalled how bad Soliz was and how far they'd come and would decide to use their change to purchase fresh water, knowing it wouldn't last longer than their exit from the city.

As they approached the corner store, just when Guadalupe feared she wouldn't have enough to nourish her family, Juanito suddenly stopped and pulled his Amá away from the beaten road.

"*¡Mira! ¡Mira!*" Juanito yelled.

Guadalupe gave a sigh of relief when he pointed to a leaky faucet on the side of a market. They bulled through the congested road, consumed with oppressed citizens, and filled their empty liters of water. Guadalupe used her large physique to cover Juanito, and because the leak was only spouting water in specks, it took minutes to fill a single bottle.

After filling all they had, they took advantage of the water and spot-rinsed themselves, while

Guadalupe thoroughly cleaned Ignacio and forced Juanito to do the same.

Guadalupe knew they had to be back on the trail before sundown, so without hesitation, they rushed through the busy slum in a panic. Although she was grateful for the fresh water, she realized that her food supply wouldn't last the night—let alone the rest of their journey.

As they continued through the slum toward the exit, Guadalupe stopped and turned back while still holding Juanito's hand.

Since the slum was populated mostly by street vendors and deprived souls, she reached into her pockets and pulled out the few pesos she had accumulated over the years from *La Chureca de Soliz*.

She counted her change at a defeated pace, resisting her tears, and instantly realized she'd never have enough to feed her flock for the duration of her journey.

She roamed the battered streets frantically, with both Juanito and Ignacio attached to her as she looked for anything possible to buy.

She might have considered begging for change, but she was surrounded by others just like her. Exhausted from her fruitless search for nutrients as the sun transitioned, they returned to the corner of the same market and prepared for another night of endurance.

***

The sky blended into the night as the town grew sparse. Guadalupe began to wilt, just as her children did on her lap. Suddenly, the soft chime of a bell and the creak of a rusted wheel woke both Guadalupe and Juanito.

Guadalupe saw a man selling food from behind a small food bike vendor just a few feet away. The man seemed to have spent his entire life behind that cart, as his skin had a similar dark char to Guadalupe.

She slowly stood and approached the vendor with both Ignacio and Juanito in hand, and asked in a broken, whimpering voice what she could buy for an entire handful of change.

The vendor looked them up and down with kind, round eyes and instantly knew from their haggard appearance that they were making the journey to *El Norte*. Without hesitation, he decided to give all he could spare.

He grabbed two stacks of flour tortillas, two other large bags of his famous black bean corn tortillas, and a couple of sweet conchas from a separate cooler attached to his bike by a red leather strap.

Then he personally handed one to Juanito and smiled. Juanito responded by saying, *"gracias"* —a smile Guadalupe hadn't seen since Ignacio's arrival months ago.

She'd thank the man and introduce herself and her children.

"Muchas gracias, este es mi hijo Juanito y mi nuevo bebé Ignacio."

"Tienes hijos preciosos. Me llamo Elian."

Guadalupe offered him her change, but he gently declined and looked at her, his eyes reflecting the pain that was all too familiar in their village.

Then, both she and Juanito walked away with renewed vigor. Before joining the trail, she handed Juanito a black bean tortilla, savoring every morsel that temporarily eased their hunger, grateful that they were beyond blessed.

CHAPTER VIII

PALE-SKINNED MEN

Days later, Guadalupe was growing weary. She was surrounded by the constant sight of exhausted journeymen and desperate children, as the once-deserted trail became overwhelmed by dreadful cries.

Determined to reach *El Norte* safely, she persisted through the crowd, knowing that talking with anyone would only distract her and hinder her chances of reaching paradise. The many stories she had heard throughout her entire life of fellow countrymen perishing before even reaching the northern border made her walk with an intense pace. Guadalupe insisted to herself that moving forward and staying strong for her children would set her apart from those who had fallen—especially Rogelio Alaniz.

Although fatigued, and scorched from her own ancestral God, a lifetime of hunger and despair prepared her well for this journey.

Guadalupe was finally beginning to feel as though she was gaining ground when she approached a famous mural she remembered hearing about as a young child—a mural of a woman with golden hair and pale skin across a brick wall.

While Juanito walked ahead, Guadalupe paused to embrace the mural's significance, and smiled. Although all that remained was an aged outline with golden and pale specs rendering her near unrecognizable, Guadalupe swelled with pride and stepped aside and continued.

Once she managed to match Juanito's pace, she felt a single raindrop graze her clenched knuckle, sending her into a slight panic.

"Juanito, ven aquí." Guadalupe said as she covered a sleeping Ignacio.

The rain turned aggressive as the desperate rushed to seek shelter, as if another setback were imminent. While a few found cover beneath makeshift shacks built mostly from rusted tin signage, most huddled under heavy branched trees that loomed over the trail.

As the once-congested path grew bare, Guadalupe pulled Juanito to her side using her bulging arm to cover him as they continued on the path. The miserable weather never fully doused her. It only fell in a light drizzle—as if they had managed to stay one step ahead of the heavy rain that others were enduring.

Slightly damp as they rushed through the trail, they'd seek shelter under a full lush tree with lengthy whipping limbs stretching towards the path as if it was waving for Guadalupe to take refuge.

Guadalupe rummaged through her belongings, pulling out plastic bags and a dingy blouse she hadn't worn since the earliest days of their journey, and used them to wrap her children for protection as tears welled on the parched ground.

The drizzle persisted as Guadalupe held her boys as tight as possible, eventually falling asleep as the rain grew into a crashing night of anger, and a symphony of blitzing lights.

***

Deep asleep, Guadalupe was abruptly awakened by the aggressive rain and the quenched sun. Ignacio remained slightly wrapped in plastic grocery bags miraculously dry from the rain. Guadalupe suddenly noticed Juanito was missing. She jolted up, alarming Ignacio, and spotted him in the distance being harassed by two older men in a black truck.

She yanked Ignacio and scurried through the forest, shouting, *"¡Juanito! ¡Juanito!"*

In defense, Guadalupe would spread herself wide while Ignacio dangled from his sling off her neck like a weathered shackle. As she lunged for Juanito, the men—one significantly taller than the other, both pale-skinned with light-colored eyes—resisted.

"¡Déjen a mi hijo en paz!" she shouted with rage and fury.

Juanito wiggled out of the men's grip and ran behind his Amá, as the pale-skinned men—dressed in dark flannel, dusty boots, and black suede vaquero hats—shouted.

"*¡Tu hijo vino a nosotros, pidiéndonos un viaje a El Norte!*" The larger vaquero said.

"*¡Está bien! ¡Estaremos bien!*" Guadalupe said seething.

"*¡Te dije que nunca nos dejaras, Juanito!*" she said sternly while yanking his arm scared and in tears.

"*Danos lo que tengas y te llevaremos hasta la frontera. Vamos en camino ahora.*" The larger pale skin man said calmly.

"*No, no, no tenemos dinero, y estamos bien.*" Guadalupe said.

"*¿Podemos al menos llevarlos al siguiente pueblo? Les daremos algo de dinero para que compren comida y alimenten a sus hijos.*" The larger man said while slowly approaching Guadalupe.

Guadalupe held Ignacio tighter as his once-comforting coos turned into harsh panting and violent kicks. At the same time, she gripped Juanito from behind, never flinching—remaining as large and imposing as possible.

"*¡No! Debemos irnos.*" Guadalupe said while back peddling never taking her eyes off the men.

A few more steps, and they slowly began to turn away.

Suddenly, she was struck from behind, collapsing and nearly falling on top of Ignacio. He screamed crying, as Juanito dropped their bags and liters of water to quickly pick up his brother and tend to their lifeless mother crying for her to wake.

The smaller man dragged both Juanito and Ignacio into the trailer of their truck with their belongings, while the large man stood over Guadalupe. As his shadow draped over her, he'd roll up his sleeves and drag her across the dusty gravel, shoving her into the back passenger side of the black truck.

***

With the sun setting, Guadalupe would be revived by deep panting from directly behind her as her body moved in cadence with the big, sweaty man on top of her back. Instead of resisting or fighting to break free, she cried out for Juanito and Ignacio, who, in turn, screamed in fear for their Amá from a distance.

Then, as if struck by the urgency of their cries, Guadalupe tried to fight off the man, but she couldn't match his strength as he persisted.

Just as she was about to give in entirely, her eyes caught something in the far corner of the truck—a rusted machete with a dirty red leather handle. She cautiously reached for it, careful not to alarm the man, when he suddenly yanked her hair and shoved her forward while still in motion.

Guadalupe grimaced in pain while discreetly reaching for the rusted machete. As she inched forward, she'd hear Ignacio and Juanito's desperate cries for *"¡Mamá!"*

A fingertips length away, she extended her calloused fingers, breathing deeply as she grazed the red leather handle.

As Guadalupe laid in painful rhythm with the pale-skinned man, she was pushed forward, able to tip the machete directly into her palm. Just as she was about to grip the handle, the pale-skinned man violently collapsed onto her back, causing her to drop the machete out of reach.

As the man's sweat dripped onto her exposed back like droplets of wax, the air from his grunts fanned her neck and right ear. Guadalupe remained stuck under the pale man's full weight as he held her down flat on her stomach with her rear pointed. She lay still in motion, gazing deeply at the machete, admiring its capabilities, as Juanito's and Ignacio's cries were suddenly drowned out by her own withering hope.

The man pushed her head down with his large hand, causing her to whimper in pain. In that moment, she noticed the letters *"R.A."* engraved just above the aged red leather handle, seemingly carved with a makeshift knife.

A sudden wave of rage filled Guadalupe, and she screamed, *"¡Ya!"* She kicked back, forcing the man to leap off her exposed body, giving her just enough time to lunge toward the machete.

In one swift motion, she grabbed the dirty red leather handle—her index finger grazing the engraved *"R.A."*—and swung the machete around her body, slicing off the man's left fingers. The man screamed to the skies and fell out of the truck, gripping his hand as blood spouted in pulses.

Guadalupe leaped onto him, driving the machete straight into his stomach with a furious scream. She yanked the red leather handle with ease and rushed toward Juanito and Ignacio, the dripping blade peppering the ground as she stood in defense, seething with fury.

The other pale man, who had been holding back Juanito, rushed toward his partner. In one swift motion, Guadalupe scooped up Ignacio and ran with Juanito to higher ground as the pale men sped away.

Both Guadalupe and Juanito watched from afar. They would then realize their bag of nourishment had been left on the truck, and all they had left was gone—along with Juanito's innocence. Guadalupe buried her head in her palms and, for the first time, cried out loud.

Juanito immediately reached for her, gently pulling her face toward his and said, *"Va a estar todo bien, Amá. No llore."*

She nodded, gave Juanito a kiss and a prayer on his forehead, and continued their walk—hoping to find anything to ease their rumbling stomachs.

As their tears tracked their miles, the closest thing they'd find were half drunken bottles of tinged water and endless debris.

***

The trail continued to grow endlessly. Guadalupe would begin to feel as if she was never gaining ground as she held onto a restless Ignacio as tightly as ever.

Meanwhile, Juanito walked ahead, defeated and unwilling to look back—perhaps afraid to see his Amá in a new light.

Although Guadalupe longed for Juanito's usual jovial spirit on the trail. In a strange way, she didn't want to see his broken eyes—because she knew he would never look at her the same.

She kept looking past Juanito in case those men came back wanting to take everything else they had. Guadalupe distinctly checked for the machete at her waist and noticed that the once-fresh blood had dried, staining the belly of the blade.

Visions of the pale-skinned man having his way with her flashed in her memory and began to overwhelm her. She desperately wanted to cry out, "*¡No!*" but knew she could never—not with Juanito.

As the memory echoed louder and louder, she accidentally tightened her grip on Ignacio, causing him to shriek deathly loud, as if he knew to cry for her.

Juanito would halt abruptly and turn back to see her for the first time since those pale men hurt his Amá. His cheeks were soaked with tears, and his eyes burned red like the aged leather handle.

Guadalupe would stop to embrace Juanito while also noticing the collar of his shirt was drenched and stretched. Overwhelmed, she sank to her knees to be eye level with him, and together they cried.

"Lo siento, mijo, no quería esto para ti."

Guadalupe clutched Juanito tightly, desperately trying to hold back her tears as both Ignacio and Juanito cried in unison.

"Está bien, sigo siendo tu mamá."

Guadalupe would look back at the battered sun, and the endless trail. Overwhelmed by their abundance she'd take a deep breath and continue.

CHAPTER IX

EERIE SILENCE

As the moon accented the sky, and the stars reigned supreme, Juanito latched onto his mom's waist as they continued in eerie silence. Although thankful for the open trail, Guadalupe grew concerned as her mind filled with images of the pale men and her children's obvious hunger. Instead of persisting through taking advantage of the empty trail until the early morning, she decided it was time to rest.

Normally, to find shelter, they would seek a large, lush tree for protection from nature.

However, the trail was lined with dried foliage and sparse brush branches that reminded her of her father's disciplinary methods as a child, so finding shelter often required both time and ingenuity.

Guadalupe swiftly turned off the trail, with Juanito still latched onto her hip, and discovered a unique shack reminiscent of her now abandoned, rusted tin-roofed home in Soliz. Although the shack was made of three weathered signages made of plywood with no front entry, it was clear the maker was on the same journey as Guadalupe—it was perfect.

Finally, covered and comfortable, Guadalupe would tell Juanito to look away as she fed Ignacio naturally. Juanito scowled in pain, clutching his stomach. While Guadalupe continued feeding Ignacio, her only thoughts were of Juanito's pain and rattling stomach.

She would rummage through her dress pockets searching for a miracle, but everything they had remained on that black truck. Frustrated, she whimpered under her breath as she turned her pockets inside out, desperately searching for anything, only to find a handful of coins earned from the landfills of Soliz. For the first time, she wished they had never left, so Juanito would be fed and not in pain.

Yet as Ignacio continued relentlessly, Guadalupe's worst fear came true as her eldest son was breaking down in hunger. She frantically searched her pockets again praying for a miracle, but found nothing.

She looked up to the stars in desperation for answers, but the wood signage was there. She'd take a deep breath and recall everything Juanito had gone through, from his life in Soliz, to Chico, and finally to the torment inflicted on her by those pale men along this journey.

She exhaled, imagining the stars beyond the makeshift roof, and called Juanito to face her.

"Mijo, mantén los ojos cerrados, por favor, y gírate hacia mí lentamente." Juanito does so.

Guadalupe sat up on her knees so she could be eye-level with him, her heartbeat echoing as if in unison with the moon's breath. She pulled him to her exposed breast and hummed an old lullaby her *Amá* used to sing, gently patting his back in rhythm with his breath—just as her *Amá* had done when she was a little girl drifting to sleep. As Juanito latched on, Guadalupe fixed her gaze on the dark corner of the shack and closed her eyes, holding back her tears until sleep eventually took her… still hungry.

CHAPTER X

THE MAGNIFICENT BEAST

The following morning, as they continued their endless journey, a drawn Juanito spotted a dark square on the horizon. He froze, as he noticed dotted colors moving, appearing suspended in the air, accompanied by rumblings that crashed through the slight breeze. Guadalupe's eyes swelled with optimism, grateful for this unexpected collage of calamity—a vivid contrast to the monotonous, dense forest and congested trail.

Juanito would eagerly sprint towards the mysterious object as Guadalupe would try to keep up, by rapidly moving her legs grazing the gravel in a low stride. As the dark, squared object became clearer and clearer, Juanito stopped dead in his tracks and waited for his Amá, who was desperately trying to keep up.

From a hill, they saw a rusted train surrounded by hungry travelers and vendors handing out food. Guadalupe's eyes swelled with optimism as she noticed many people gathered atop the train's roof. She recalled having heard of a passing train, though all she knew was that it was dangerous and diverted passengers along a different route—one that avoided the dreadful, dense desert she desperately hoped to elude.

Before approaching the train, and what seemed like a land of weary travelers, Guadalupe quickly fed Ignacio along the lonely trail.

They approached the sleeping behemoth from the hill, Guadalupe noticed a small town east of the train. While walking, she considered detouring into the neighboring town to take the long way *Norte*, presumably leading directly through the desert, but when she saw food being handed out to people like her and Juanito, she chose instead to step forward.

Amongst the dense hungry crowd consumed with cries of exhaust and the unknown, Juanito would latch onto his mother's waist like that day after the pale-skinned men took advantage of his Amá and walk amongst them. In that moment, she realized that the souls and love of every traveler had been replaced with hope and hunger, as they bobbed and weaved through the masses.

She also saw children, some younger than Juanito and others scarcely older than Ignacio, wandering alone, lost and crying with a sense of horror and abandonment that she could never imagine for her own children, but knew she was among them.

Despite the stench of despair, Guadalupe noticed a spark of community, as some reached out to help feed others, while many remained trapped in the crowd and others pressed forward in search of the land of prosperity, she so desperately desired.

She stopped in front of the beastly train, noticing people crowded atop its rooftops. From the chaotic whispers of the crowd, she'd gathered that it wasn't set to depart until the following morning. Guadalupe grabbed the hard-rusted side ladder, testing if she could muster enough strength to pull herself up. She handed Ignacio to Juanito, who kissed his own sunburnt, dried forehead before lifting him. Her foot stayed planted as her calloused palm began to tear.

Sizing up the ladder once more, Guadalupe summoned every ounce of her strength and, with a full-body heave, barely managed to lift herself against its side. Suddenly, she jumped off and landed violently on her knees as the passing travelers rushed to help. She waved them away in frustration, determined to stand on her own and dust off her knees that dripped with blood.

"Vamos a tener que despertar temprano para que pueda pedir ayuda, o si no, tendremos que esperar al próximo tren."

Guadalupe looked along the length of the train, which seemed as endless as the trail they'd walked. Feeling helpless, she returned Ignacio to his sling.

She wandered toward the back and noticed an old concrete train stop that had been hollowed out into a three-walled shelter—a refuge where everyone sought shade while awaiting the next train.

Exhausted, she sat against the corner of the wall. When someone greeted her with food and a bag of tortillas, she felt more grateful than she had since Elian. As dusk settled and everyone was well fed, Guadalupe guarded Ignacio while keeping a nervous eye on Juanito, who joyfully played fútbol with a crushed tin can alongside other hopeful spirits—playing their game steps away from the magnificent beast.

The day's heat lingered into the night, mingling with the resting bodies' warmth as Guadalupe cradled her sleeping children amid the bedlam of hopeful travelers, while the luminous moon provided a ghastly silhouette over the cold steel monster looming above the sweltering shelter.

Guadalupe remained on alert as she overheard dreadful stories of people losing limbs while trying to climb the roof of a moving train. She also learned that the morning train would be the last of the season.

Throughout the night, Guadalupe remained restless, haunted by the screams of lost children calling for their *"mamas" y "papas"*, a sound that made her weep quietly while her precious seeds slept peacefully. Unable to gaze upon the stars, she instead admired the cracked, hardened trail etched into the concrete wall she leaned against and whispered a silent prayer. Eventually, Juanito awoke without moving from her lap as she ran her fingers through his coarse hair, staying alert.

Whenever strange men passed by, Guadalupe grew nervous, often trembling with fear that the pale-skinned men might return. She reached around her waist to hold the machete, startling Juanito. He suddenly lunged around his Amá's arm and pulled out the machete like a knight.

Surprised by his own actions, he looked directly into her eyes and, with calm determination, said,

"Déjame protegerte, Amá."

His presence calmed Guadalupe as she watched her firstborn son turn into a man. While he remained alert and ready, a quiet sense of peace absorbed her. Eventually, her eyes grew heavy as Juanito stood guard.

***

Guadalupe was suddenly awakened by a piercing whistle and a stampede of desperate travelers, all hopeful of boarding the slow-moving beast.

She jolted up and rushed toward the train, startling Ignacio, who cried out in a trembling, shrieking murmur. She pushed Juanito forward, guiding him through the chaos as if they were parting through a sea of humans.

From a distance, Guadalupe saw frantic bodies, both of older children and young children, climbing atop the obtuse titan as if it were second nature.

While most ascended directly onto the rooftop, many extended their arms from the train's ladders, desperately pulling up their brethren, as though the train had spouted hundreds of hardened, burnt tentacles. Deafening cries echoed amid the chaos, as many were swallowed underneath by the hungry behemoth, its momentum fueled by their desperation.

Within moments, Guadalupe and Juanito came within reach of a young man and woman whose outstretched hands promised help. While frantic, Guadalupe pushed Juanito forward as he pulled himself onto the train with surprising ease.

Immediately, Juanito turned back, calling out for his Amá, crying as he urged a nearby man to extend his hand and help her.

The train began to accelerate, and for the first time since childhood, Guadalupe found herself running. Her hand, outstretched in desperate hope for someone to lift them, trembled as her fear turned to hopelessness.

Amongst the mayhem, she removed Ignacio from his soiled sling—a move that slowed her considerably—in hopes that someone might save him and miraculously reunite him with Juanito.

As her mouth fumbled with cries of desperation, Guadalupe stretched her arm fully—just inches from letting Ignacio go—when her foot caught on uneven gravel.

She tumbled hard to the ground, still miraculously clutching her baby, as the train thundered away.

Guadalupe sat up gasping for breath and instinctively rubbed Ignacio's blood-speckled face, crying out for Juanito as she would hear his voice from a distance, *"¡Ama! ¡Ignacio!"* Guadalupe looked beyond the dust from her violent fall and saw the same man and woman holding back Juanito as he struggled to jump off the fleeing beast before it vanished into the dark tunnel.

She cried out to the gray skies, *"¡JUANITO!"* and wept over the battered Ignacio, who remained paralyzed as the train disappeared. As she clutched him, memories flashed through her mind—his birth, the first time she fed Juanito, and the moment she heard him cry, *"¡Amá!*

Then, as she collapsed onto her back, she realized that Juanito's cry for her would be the last sound she would ever hear from him. In that final moment, she bellowed deep into the belly of Ignacio.

***

Hours passed as Guadalupe prayed that Juanito would emerge from the dark tunnel, but he never did. With her face powdered by dust, she mustered the strength to stand, her eyes fixed on that ominous opening. Her bottom lip hung, cut and still wet with blood that had blended with her tears.

Unsure of what to do next, she considered waiting for the next train, where at least she'd be fed and sheltered, but the haunted memories of voided faces, sobbing screams, the stench of crushed bones, and traces of sandy blood proved too unbearable to endure again.

Consumed by the loss of her first son, she clung to the fragile hope that he might one day reach the other side. That hope drove her to press onward, moving north through the desert, yearning to hear Juanito call out *"¡Amá!"* once more.

Guadalupe eventually made her way back to the train stop, now once again bursting with dread—and with wounded, bereaved souls like her and Ignacio. She was greeted by loving people who understood her loss without asking, as if they had seen her pain time and time again. She'd be given plenty of nourishment as she would tell her plans to keep going to *El Norte* to be reunited with Juanito.

She was told the only way to paradise was through the desert. With love, they warned her: the desert was where most lives were claimed— it was a stretch that would determine her fate. Glancing back toward the tunnel where Juanito had disappeared, she imagined holding him once more. Then, as a cool breeze caressed her face, she stepped forward.

CHAPTER XI

THE MEN IN GREEN JACKETS

Guadalupe walked with one foot dragging over the parched sands, clutching her left side while supporting an unkempt Ignacio—weeks after leaving Juanito behind. Determined to see him again, she pressed on relentlessly, feeding Ignacio along the way.

As the weeks passed, Ignacio seemed to age before her eyes as his skin had darkened, and Guadalupe was forced to transition from breastfeeding as her breasts had grown tender. At night, as she rested with Ignacio, their cries for

Juanito echoed in unison, strangely keeping the lurking wildlife at bay.

Her only respite in the endless desert came when she reached up to her waist and discovered that the machete was gone—a bittersweet realization that brought a grateful smile to her face, evoking memories of her eldest son growing into a man. In that silent moment, she prayed that he would never have to use it.

The beige desert slowly blended into a medley of emerald brush as the sifting silence of the grainy hills was overwhelmed by the crashing of the nearby river. Guadalupe sensed she was close to paradise, and possibly to Juanito—as his voice consumed her.

As the glistening horizon became true and the high streams revealed a man-made casting shadow, tears trickled down her cheeks. For the first time since the steel mammoth stole her first love, she picked up her feet. Just steps from the river, she stopped abruptly to take in a deep breath.

She approached with caution, where the divide between death and paradise was consumed with hostile currents and violent streams—she'd wipe away her tears. Guadalupe turned back to see an imprinted trail stretched thin into the sandy gravel. She inhaled the welcoming border winds, causing her to grin gratefully for what she had endured and all she had lost. Looking down at Ignacio, she wept, thankful for his strength and smile.

They were a single crossing away from accomplishing what no one from Soliz had ever done, now standing at the threshold of life for the first time. She turned to face the murky streams of the high tide and look past them. Though the rugged terrain mirrored the hardships she had endured, she knew it led straight to Eden and perhaps, one day, into the arms of Juanito.

She looked back once more at a cooing Ignacio and smiled, realizing his journey had only just begun, and that one day, he would have the chance to tell his own story.

Guadalupe waited for the raging tide to calm—but it never did. The moon's reflection illuminated the river entirely, as the streams continued to run amuck. With Ignacio fed, she stepped toward the water to wash. Though she had rinsed herself sporadically throughout her journey, it only been in fleeting moments, never enough to feel truly cleansed.

She slipped off her torn sandals, dipping her wounded feet slightly moaning from its welcomed cool relief. As the river embraced her, she reached for an empty water bottle, discarded in the desert by kind humanitarians, and rinsed Ignacio in what had seemed days.

She stared, frozen. Embarrassed, she hadn't realized she had never fully cleaned the dried remnants of the pale-skinned man's violence weeks ago. A wave of shame washed over her.

Yet, as she stood beneath the pure light of the full moon, she pressed her trembling fingers to her chest and made the sign of the cross—grateful to be alive for this moment of cleansing under the full moon.

Guadalupe nods off with Ignacio asleep on her lap, her feet still submerged in the river. Suddenly, a sharp beam of light pierced through the darkness and into her eyes.

Blinded by the glare, she struggled to stand as Ignacio screeched in agony. As her vision sharpened, she saw men in green jackets slam their truck into park, as a stern voice pierced through a speaker,

"*¡Quieto!*"

Guadalupe pressed her palm over Ignacio's trembling mouth, scurrying toward the low brush and the roaring river.

"*¡No! ¡Por favor!*" she cried as the large men in green advanced. She darted a desperate glance between the furious waters and the approaching figures—there was no escape.

As they closed in, she took a slow, deliberate step into the river, lifting her last son high above her, toward heaven. Inch by inch, the raging currents swallowed her, rising past her shoulders with each step. The men in green shouted,

"*¡Sal de ahí! ¡El río es peligroso! ¡Por favor, regresa!*"

But she persisted. The crushing streams wilted her balance as she inched closer and closer to paradise. The freezing water bobbed up and down against her face. Her elbows would begin to bend as she pushed forward in horror, the men in green jackets still yelling,

"*¡Regresa!*"

With their pistols now at attention. Guadalupe bulled forward with her knees blasting in and out contradicting the swift currents as the cold water receded from her chin. Just as she was about to claim new land, she struck uneven ground.

In an instant, she plunged beneath the dark river. She surfaced with a gasp—Ignacio was gone. Frozen, she strained to hear him crying, but there was nothing—only the men in green shouting, threatening to, *"¡Dispara!"* if she crossed over.

Panicked, Guadalupe dove back into the river, hands clawing through the black water. Nothing. She thrashed through the high grass at the river's edge, desperate, hopeful—but he was gone. The violent current had swallowed him whole.

She screamed in raw, shattered desperation, over and over, her cries piercing through the night. The men in green covered their ears, wincing at the unbearable grief. She had lost both of her reasons to live.

Frantic, she pulled herself to shore, still searching, still hoping—blaming herself for ever challenging the great *Marcha de la Muerte*. She never even realized she was feet into *El Norte*. Suddenly, she was tackled to the ground.

CHAPTER XII

A SOULLESS WHITE SHROUD

As soft whimpers purred through the loose gravel of Soliz, Guadalupe sat outside her rusted tin shack, gazing up at the same inspirational stars—shimmering like tears.

She looked down, rocking back and forth, cradling Juanito's still body. He lay wrapped in a soulless white shroud, stained with burgundy spots. Juanito's face was unrecognizable, ravaged by the wild. Yet she knew him—not by his burrowed eyes, nor his torn lips, but by the birthmark on his cheek—the only part of him untouched by nature. Gently, she traced it with her trembling scarred fingers, as her tears fell onto him like heavy rain filling a well.

Stricken with grief, she'd survey her barrio, realizing she was never meant to leave—and wished she never had. Her gaze drifted to the machete leaning against the tin door. She stared at its aged red leather handle, the weight of its presence settling over her as she now understood that her new pain was now forever.

As the moon sank into the horizon, Guadalupe's tears dried. She remained frozen, staring at her now lifeless son as she cradled the left side of her belly. Just as she began to wonder what her purpose was, she looked down, startled, to see two ants crawling over the charred hump of her foot, marching forward onto an endless trail.

Guadalupe then looked back up to the stars.

www.ingramcontent.com/pod-product-compliance
Lightning Source LLC
Chambersburg PA
CBHW030417120726
47904CB00007B/2313